This is for the ones who want to speak the truth,
the ones doing the hard and sacred work of nurturing
young minds into beautiful human beings…the teachers. —K.A.

To Mom, Shay, Sisi, Dad, Ron, Antt with two Ts, Holly Fischer,
Michael S. Williams and the Black on Black Project, Terri Dollar,
April May, Rubin, of course, Kwame for certain, and everyone else whose
love and support it took to get me here! Thank you! —Dare

# AN AMERI

Kwame Alexander ★ Art by Dare Coulter

# CAN STORY

LITTLE, BROWN AND COMPANY
New York   Boston

How do you tell a story
that starts in Africa
and ends in horror?

An unbelievable story
about evil plans
and big guns
hiding
in the night

waiting

while the girls
and the boys
finish chores
play games
listen to old tales
of trickster spiders
and talking drums

waiting

for the women
to sing everyone
to sleep,
for the men
to dream
of tomorrow

waiting

to steal them away
from their lives
and sell them
in America.

But you can't sell people.

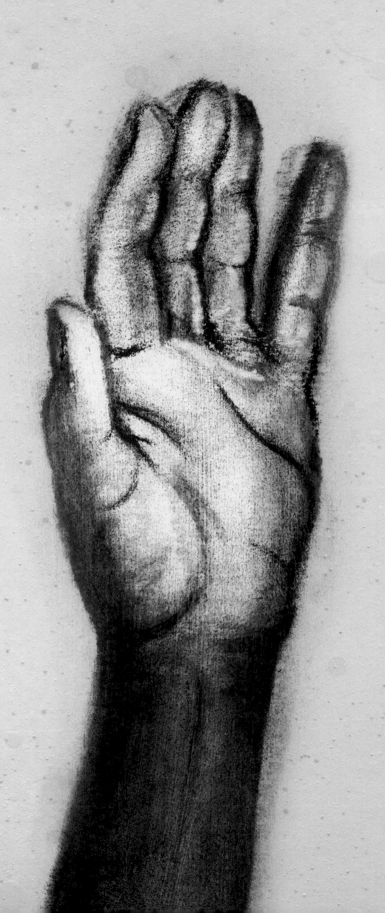

How do you tell a story about slavery?

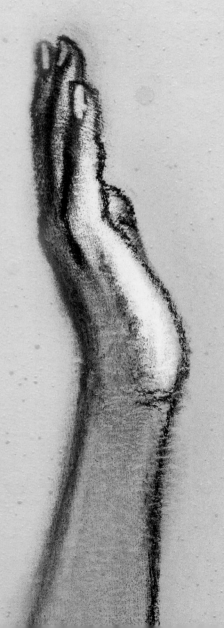

About sly men
from cold places
scheming
and laughing
on tall ships…

while people
shackled below,
crammed in
small, hot spaces,
cry and
sometimes die.

A story
of struggle
and sacrifice
about bold men
and women
jumping
into the sea,
into the jaws
of sharks
because—

They were scared and didn't know where they were being taken?

Or what they'd find when they got there?

Maybe they just wanted to escape.

How do you tell that story?
About copper dreams
wrapped in iron chains.

About working hard
for long hours,
from can see
to can't.

For free.

About picking cotton
and growing sugar
under the burning sun

while blond-haired boys
and girls
ate their candy
and played tag
before school
in their woolen breeches
and cotton gowns.

And no reading ALLOWED.

And no reading ALOUD.

About planting corn
And threshing rice
And curing tobacco
And harvesting coffee

And cooking
And cleaning
And building

FOR FREE.

Why weren't they paid?

That's not fair.

How do you tell a story
about strength
and pride
and refusing
to be broken

and refusing
to stop smiling
and loving

and each night
gathering the children
by the fire
to hear tales
of Moses
and trickster rabbits
and missing home

And missing home.

*That's sad. Really, really sad, Ms. Simmons.*

How do you tell that story and not want to weep for the world?

A story about mothers
fleeing in the wind
wading in the water
conducting freedom.

About fathers
fighting back
stealing away
chasing liberty.

About some being caught
by the searing lash
of night riders

and others riding the night
by the light
of the North Star.

About little girls
waking up
in the middle of the night
to their tormented mothers pleading
*Please don't take my boy from me.*

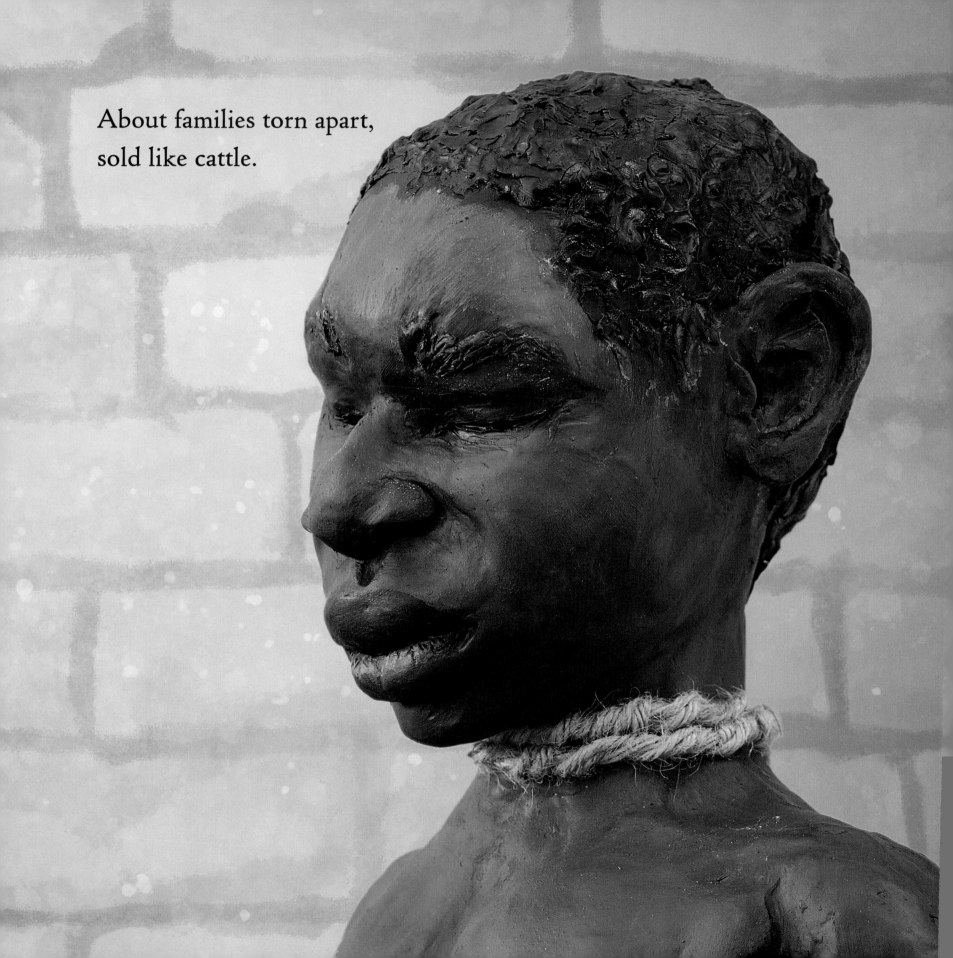

About families torn apart,
sold like cattle.

I don't think I can continue.
It's just too painful.
I shouldn't have read this
to you. I'm so sorry, children.

But, don't you tell us to always speak the truth, Ms. Simmons, even when it's hard?

When I've done something bad, my dad always says, "You can't change the past, but you can do better in the future."

Whenever I'm sad, my grandma sings me her favorite poem: "We've suffered, been battered, our lives have been scattered, but we're still here. And that's all that matters. We're still here."

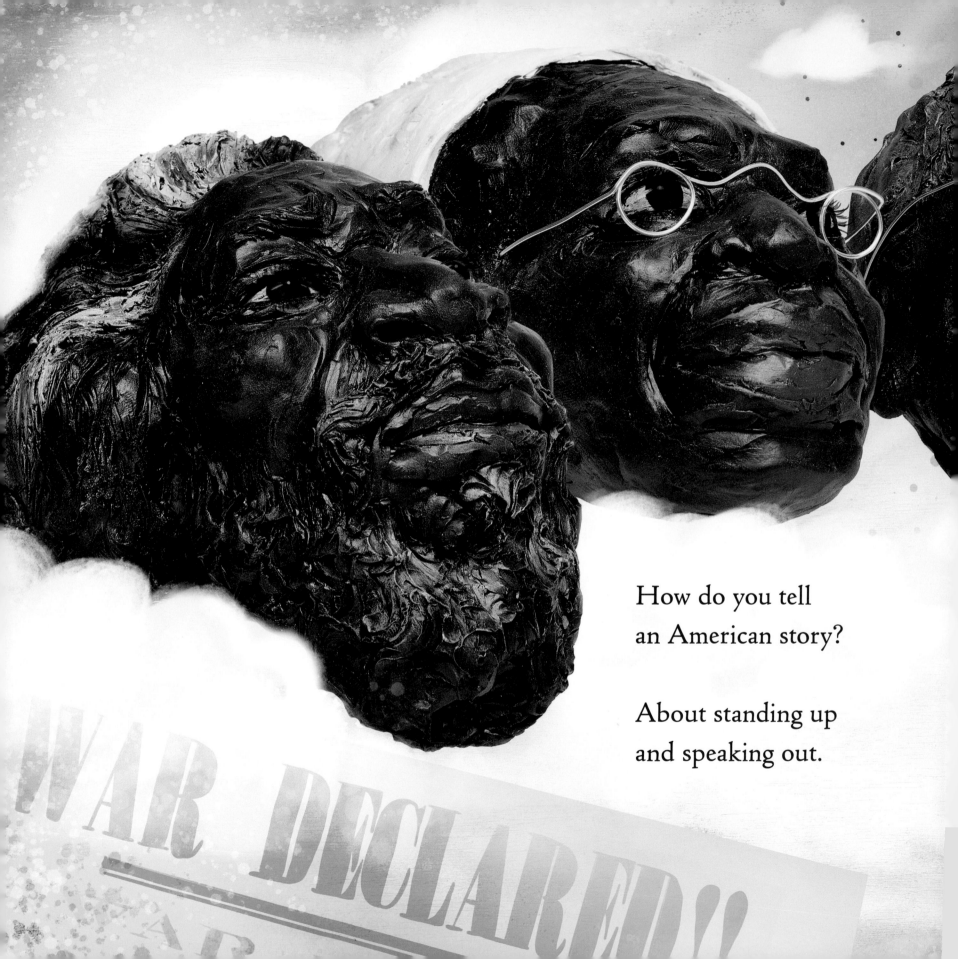

How do you tell
an American story?

About standing up
and speaking out.

About Sojourner Truth
and Robert Smalls.

About the Civil War
and emancipation.

About yesterday's nightmare
and the courage to dream
a new tomorrow.

How do you tell a story
this hard to hear,
one that hurts
and still loves?

You do it
by being brave enough
to lift your voice,

by holding
history
in one hand

and clenching
hope
in the other.

## A NOTE FROM THE AUTHOR

I wrote this story after a racially charged incident happened in my daughter's fourth grade classroom. They were learning about life in the thirteen colonies without discussing the impact and trauma of slavery. During a parent-teacher conference to discuss the matter, my daughter's teacher became defensive, distressed. We realized that her anxiety came from a fear of teaching slavery, which stemmed from the fact that she was never taught how to teach slavery in the classroom. It became apparent that so many schools don't prepare their students to fully understand the truth about slavery. Because it's scary. And hard. I believe *An American Story* can help give us a way to speak the truth to children, so we can all stop being afraid, so we can start moving closer to our better selves.

## A NOTE FROM THE ILLUSTRATOR

Most of my work focuses on joy, but this book deals with difficult and painful subjects, and I wanted to make sure to do the history justice. I researched for weeks, though at points I had to stop because of the horror of what I was reading. But while researching I also learned about places like the kingdom of Benin and how amazing it was before it was destroyed. I hunted for details like the layouts of cargo ships, fabric and indigo processes in precolonial Africa, and how things like lights, clothing, and kitchens would have worked on plantations.

Next was creating the artwork. Half of the sculptures are water-based clay that is fired in a kiln, and the rest are polymer clay that gets baked in a regular kitchen oven. The paintings are acrylic and spray paint on wood panel, and the drawings are charcoal on gessoed paper. Once everything was finished, I packed it all into a car and drove from North Carolina to Brooklyn, New York, to have the pieces photographed.

One of my favorite spreads references the Gullah Geechee (shown harvesting rice), who most successfully preserved the culture of *home* upon being stolen from their ancestral lands and brought to the American South. It's both inspiring and sad, as the theft of a people never should have happened. The Gullah Geechee heritage is a reminder of the resilience and brilliance of our people, but it's also living proof that the institution of slavery and the decimation of a continent for the sake of profit really did happen. This book is a reminder that there is a wrong to be righted, even if it's complicated and takes a long time. The process of making this book has taken nearly six years.

I'd like to thank: my dear agent, Rubin Pfeffer, who was hip and hip with me through this three-legged race—I'm forever grateful to you; the fiercely talented C, who opened this door for me; Bo12, who pushed me to be and do better; Charles B, Anne McLean, Katina Parker, Devin Lafluer, and Val and Joose, who got me through this and last year; Whitney Leader-Picone, who so lovingly raised this book; Saho, Dave, and Margaret—finishing this journey with you was amazing; Howard Huang, thanks for the magic of your studio—your photos brought the sculptures to life; and Kwame, thank you for your brilliance and the blessing of this manuscript—I rock with you forever! Mommy, we're finally flying!

## ABOUT THIS BOOK

The illustrations in this book are mixed-media and were created with a combination of spray paint, acrylic paint, charcoal, graphite, ink, and digital painting on wood panel and watercolor paper, and also using Procreate and Adobe Photoshop. The sculptures are both ceramic and polymer clay with added materials and were painted with acrylic paint and spray paint. This book was edited by Margaret Raymo and designed by Patrick Collins with art direction from Whitney Leader-Picone and Saho Fujii. The production was supervised by Lillian Sun, and the production editor was Andy Ball. The text was set in Cloister and Gill Sans, and the display type is Valfieris Aged.